Hello, Family Members,

Learning to read is one of the most important accomplishments of early childhood. **Hello Reader!** books are designed to help children become skilled readers  beginning readers learn to read by remembering frequently used words like "the," "is," and "and"; by using phonics skills to decode new words; and by interpreting picture and text clues. These books provide both the stories children enjoy and the structure they need to read fluently and independently. Here are suggestions for helping your child *before*, *during*, and *after* reading:

Before
- Look at the cover and pictures and have your child predict what the story is about.
- Read the story to your child.
- Encourage your child to chime in with familiar words and phrases.
- Echo read with your child by reading a line first and having your child read it after you do.

During
- Have your child think about a word he or she does not recognize right away. Provide hints such as "Let's see if we know the sounds" and "Have we read other words like this one?"
- Encourage your child to use phonics skills to sound out new words.
- Provide the word for your child when more assistance is needed so that he or she does not struggle and the experience of reading with you is a positive one.
- Encourage your child to have fun by reading with a lot of expression . . . like an actor!

After
- Have your child keep lists of interesting and favorite words.
- Encourage your child to read the books over and over again. Have him or her read to brothers, sisters, grandparents, and even teddy bears. Repeated readings develop confidence in young readers.
- Talk about the stories. Ask and answer questions. Share ideas about the funniest and most interesting characters and events in the stories.

I do hope that you and your child enjoy this book.

—Francie Alexander
Reading Specialist,
Scholastic's Learning Ventures

To my wife, artistic partner, and best friend Alice

—P.S.

ISBN 0-439-20473-9

Text copyright © 2000 by Stephanie Calmenson.
Illustrations copyright © 2000 by Paul and Alice Sharp.
All rights reserved. Published by Scholastic Inc.
SCHOLASTIC, HELLO READER, CARTWHEEL BOOKS and associated logos are
trademarks and/or registered trademarks of Scholastic Inc.

Library of Congress Cataloging-in-Publication Data

Calder, Lyn.
    What's my job? / by Lyn Calder ; illustrated by Paul and Alice Sharp.
        p.   cm.— (Hello reader! Level 1)
    "Cartwheel Books."
    Summary: Brief rhyming clues invite the reader to identify a variety of occupations.
    ISBN 0-439-20473-9 (pbk.)
    [1. Occupations—Fiction. 2. Stories in rhyme.] I.Sharp, Alice, ill. II. Sharp, Paul, ill.
III. Title. IV. Series.
PZ8.3.C13 Wf 2000
[E]—dc21   00-020343

15 14 13   08

Printed in the U.S.A.   23
First printing, October 2000

What's My Job?

by Lyn Calder
Illustrated by Paul and Alice Sharp

Hello Reader!—Level 1

SCHOLASTIC INC.
New York   Toronto   London   Auckland   Sydney
Mexico City   New Delhi   Hong Kong

"All aboard!"
is what I say.
Then I take your ticket
and we're on our way.

Who am I?

Train conductor.

See my shiny red truck.
Hear my sirens blast!
When a house is on fire,
I get there fast!

Who am I?

Firefighter.

If you are lost,
come look for me.
My badge and uniform
are easy to see.

Who am I?

Police officer.

Your nose can tell you
the things that I make:
bread, muffins, and pies,
buns, cookies, and cake.

Who am I?

Baker.

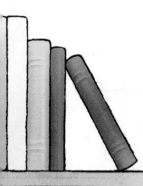

Are you looking for a book
to read?
Here are many, old and new.
I can help you borrow some.
Please return them when
they're due.

BOOK

RETURN

Who am I?

Librarian.

Whatever the weather,
sun, rain, or snow,
I deliver your letters
wherever they go.

Who am I?

Letter carrier.

I move in time to music.
I will show you how.
Step, leap, tap, twirl!
Now I'll take my bow.

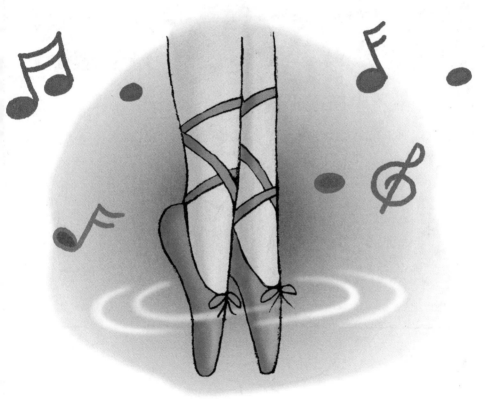

Who am I?

Dancer.

Watch my tall black hat
as I wave my wand about.
"Abracadabra!"
A white rabbit pops out!

Who am I?

Magician.

Climb aboard my yellow bus.
We'll ride to school and then,
when your school day's over,
I'll drive you home again.

Who am I?

School bus driver.

I greet you in your classroom when the school bell rings. I'm always there to help you, so you can learn new things.

Who am I?

Teacher.

Is your hair getting shaggy?
Come in, take a seat.
I'll cut it and comb it
to make it look neat.

Who am I?

Haircutter.

I look at your teeth
to make sure they are all right.
Then I give you a toothbrush
to help keep them bright.

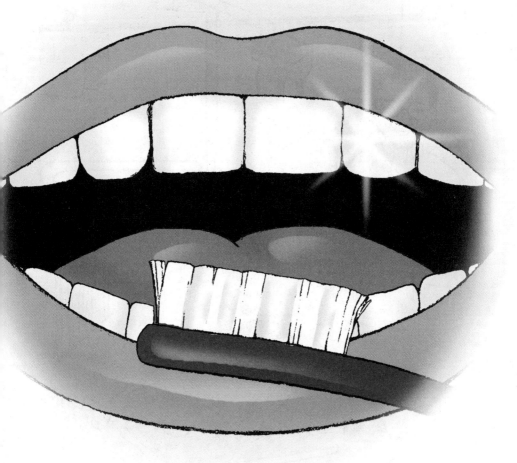

Who am I?

Dentist.

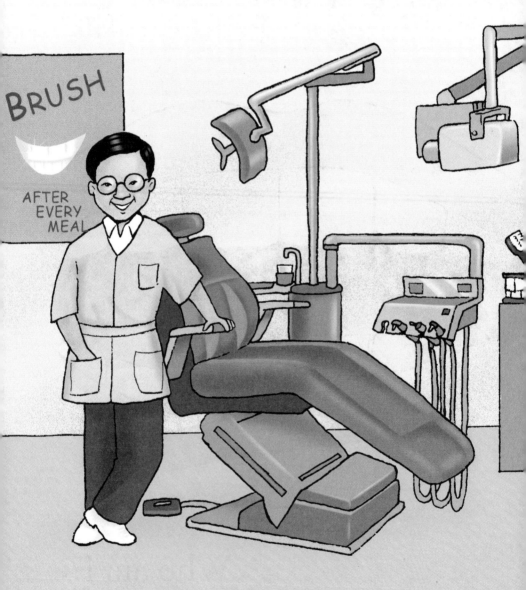

Come visit me
when you feel sick.
I will try to help you
get well quick.

Who am I?

Doctor.

Since you came into our lives,
we've watched you grow.
We love you so much.
Who are we? Do you know?

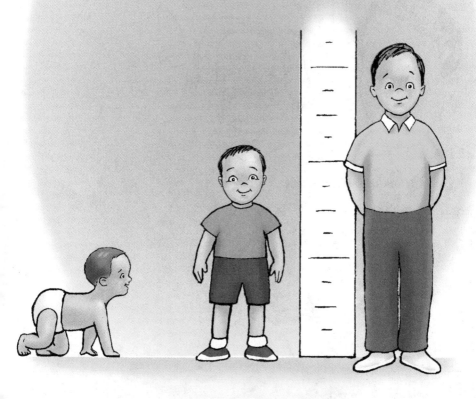

Family.